Wolves

Written by Carol Krueger

These animals are wolves.
Look at their fur coats.

They have two coats.
They have an inside coat
to keep them warm.
They have an outside coat
to keep them dry.

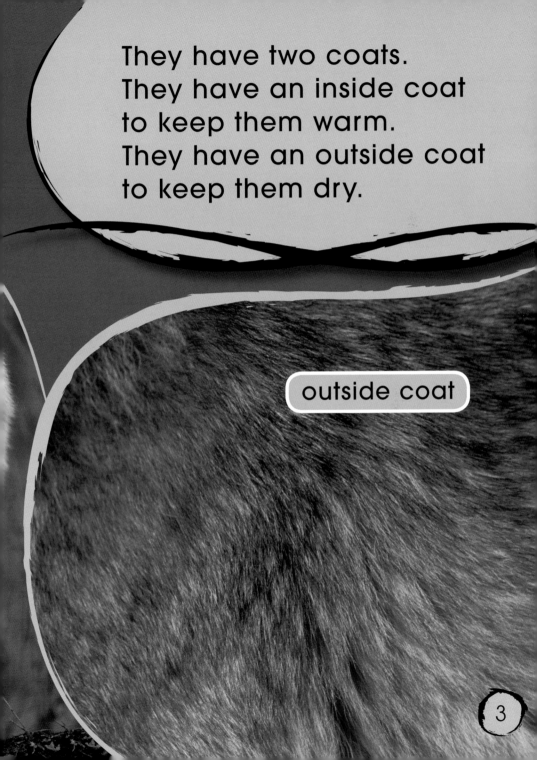

outside coat

Wolves howl at night.
They are telling other wolves
to stay away.
They are very loud.
You can hear them howling
from a long way away!

Wolves howl when
they are hunting for food, too.
They do not hunt alone.
They hunt with their family.
They howl to the other wolves
in their family.

The wolf family
is called a pack.
There can be eight wolves
in a pack.

A wolf will help
the other wolves in the pack.
These wolves are hunting
in the snow.
They run in a line.
They make tracks
in the snow for
the other wolves to see.

tracks

9

This wolf is looking for food
under the snow.
Wolves have very good noses.
They can smell food
from a long way away.

Wolves have long legs.
They can hunt animals
that run very fast.
The wolves must run very fast
to catch them.

Wolves are wild animals.
They stay away from people,
and people stay away from them.
But these people are helping
a sick wolf.

Index

15

▬▬▬ **Guide Notes**

Title: Wolves
Stage: Early (4) – Green

Genre: Nonfiction
Approach: Guided Reading
Processes: Thinking Critically, Exploring Language, Processing Information
Written and Visual Focus: Photographs (static images), Labels, Index
Word Count: 201

THINKING CRITICALLY
(sample questions)
- Look at the front cover and the title. Ask the children what they know about wolves.
- Look at the title and read it to the children.
- Focus the children's attention on the index. Ask: "What are you going to find out about in this book?"
- If you want to find out about why wolves howl, what pages would you look on?
- If you want to find out about how wolves hunt, what pages would you look on?
- Look at page 9. Why do you think the wolves run in a single line in the snow?
- Look at page 14. What do you think might have happened to the sick wolf and why do you think the people want to help it?

EXPLORING LANGUAGE

Terminology
Title, cover, photographs, author, photographers

Vocabulary
Interest words: wolf, coat, howl, pack
High-frequency words: keep, called, must
Positional words: inside, outside, in, under
Compound words: inside, outside

Print Conventions
Capital letter for sentence beginnings, periods, commas, exclamation mark